IN THE FOOTSTEPOCK HOLMES

THE C
SILENT CANARY

*A new Sherlock Holmes story based on the
notebooks and papers of John H. Watson MD*

Written and Researched by
ALLEN SHARP

Cambridge University Press
Cambridge
New York   Port Chester   Melbourne   Sydney

In the footsteps of Sherlock Holmes
The Case of the Baffled Policeman
The Case of the Buchanan Curse
The Case of the Devil's Hoofmarks
The Case of the Frightened Heiress
The Case of the Gentle Conspirators
The Case of the Howling Dog
The Case of the Man who Followed Himself
The Case of the Silent Canary

Published by the Press Syndicate of the University of Cambridge
The Pitt Building, Trumpington Street, Cambridge CB2 1RP
40 West 20th Street, New York, NY 10011, USA
10 Stamford Road, Oakleigh, Melbourne 3166, Australia

First published 1990

Printed in Great Britain by the Guernsey Press Co. Ltd, Guernsey

British Library cataloguing in publication data
Sharp, Allen
The case of the silent canary – (Sharp, Allen. In the
footsteps of Sherlock Holmes).
1. Title
823'.914[F]

ISBN 0 521 38957 7

DS

The cover photograph is reproduced with permission from
City of Westminster: Sherlock Holmes Collection, Marylebone Library
The picture frame was loaned by Tobiass.
pp.11 and 36 by Celia Hart, p.47 © Museum of London

The author wishes to acknowledge the indispensable
assistance which has been afforded by frequent reference
to the considerable earlier work of the late
Sir Arthur Conan Doyle.

About the Series

In 1881, Sherlock Holmes, while working in the chemical laboratory of St Bartholomew's hospital in London, met Dr John Watson, an army surgeon recently returned to England. Watson was looking for lodgings. Holmes had just found some which were too large for his needs, and wanted someone to share the rent. So it was that Holmes and Watson moved into 221B Baker Street. It was the beginning of a partnership which was to last more than twenty years and one which would make 221B Baker Street one of the most famous addresses in all of England.

Some credit for that partnership must also go to Mrs Hudson, Sherlock Holmes' landlady and housekeeper. It was she who put up with a lodger who made awful smells with his chemical experiments, who played the violin at any time of the day or night, who kept cigars in the coal scuttle, and who pinned his letters to the wooden mantlepiece with the blade of a knife!

So it is perhaps not unfitting that the only original documents which are known to have survived from those twenty years are now owned by Mrs Susan Stacey, a grandniece of that same Mrs Hudson. They include three of Dr Watson's notebooks or, more accurately, two notebooks and a diary which has been used as a notebook. The rest is an odd assortment, from letters and newspaper clippings to photographs and picture postcards. The whole collection has never been seen as anything more than a curiosity. The notebooks do not contain any complete accounts of cases – only jottings – though some of these were very probably made on the spot in the course of actual investigations. Occasionally, something has been pinned or pasted to a page of a notebook. There are some rough sketches and, perhaps the most interesting, there are many ideas and questions which Watson must have noted down so that he could discuss them with Holmes at some later time.

But now, by using Watson's notebooks, old newspaper reports, police files, and other scraps of information which the documents provide, it has been possible to piece together some of Holmes' cases which have never before been published. In each story, actual pages from the notebooks, or other original documents, have been included. They will be found in places where they add some information, provide some illustration, or pick out what may prove to be important clues.

But it is hoped that they also offer something more. By using your imagination, these pages can give **you** the opportunity to relive the challenge, the excitement and, occasionally, the danger which Watson, who tells the stories, must himself have experienced in working with Sherlock Holmes – the man so often described as "the world's greatest detective".

Chapter One

The Dynamiters

On the morning of Saturday May 31st 1884, breakfast at 221B Baker Street was interrupted by the arrival of a breathless and very-young-looking police constable. He carried a note for Sherlock Holmes. Since the young man appeared somewhat uncertain as to whether the note required an immediate reply, Holmes insisted upon his waiting in our rooms until he had read it.

"It's from Inspector Sweeny," Holmes told me. "He's the assistant to Chief Inspector Littlechild – the man who Monro recently assigned to take charge of the Special Irish Branch. The note is to inform me that between the hours of nine and ten last night there were a number of explosions in Westminster. All, it seems, were in St James's Square, with the exception of one. That occurred at Scotland Yard itself."

"Good heavens!" I said. "With what damage or loss of life?"

"The note does not tell us either, Watson. Perhaps the constable can."

"I can just tell you what I heard, sir," was his reply. "I'm from A Division, you see."

"So you're stationed at King Street."

"Yes, sir. It's when I reports there for duty at eight o'clock this morning, my sergeant gives me this note and tells me to bring it here. He says that Inspector Sweeny's one of them whose offices was blew up. He didn't think he was in it at the time, it being about half past nine at night when it happened."

"And that's all you know?" Holmes asked.

"The sergeant did say it was a bad one. He says there's not a pane of glass left in the Rising Sun – it being just across the road. He says that it shifted the beer engine and that Daisy Collins was awful cut about the neck with the flying glass."

"Daisy Collins?"

"The barmaid sir."

"I see. Thank you, constable. There is no reply. And should anyone ask, I've no doubt that Dr Watson and myself will be visiting the scene later this morning."

Holmes saw the constable down the stairs to the street door realising, I think, that I was having some difficulty in restraining my laughter. His own face had a broad grin upon it when he returned.

"A useful reminder, Watson," he said, "that all of us do not have the same priorities. Our constable does perhaps represent an extreme example, but how often have I listened to a seemingly well-observed account from which the most vital detail has been totally omitted. And it was not because the witness had failed to observe it, but because that witness had not considered it of any importance. But I do believe that I hear Mrs Hudson with breakfast, which I do not intend to hurry unduly. As twelve hours have elapsed since the events of last evening, I doubt whether one more will make a significant difference. What evidence might have been visible is now most probably gone – if not swept away, then trodden under the feet of a curious public."

....

Despite the brief amusement afforded by the young constable, the news we had received that morning was undoubtedly serious. Fuller and more reliable detail was hardly necessary to assume that, apart from damage to property, there must have been many injuries, even possibly deaths. In the event it transpired that there were no deaths, but a policeman and the driver of a brougham that was standing in Great Scotland Yard at the time of the explosion were severely injured, and very many persons both in the vicinity of the Yard and in St James's Square were badly lacerated by flying glass.

Those responsible for the events of last evening, were an organisation known as *The Fenian Brotherhood*, a group of Irish Americans whose aim was to overthrow the English domination of Ireland and make it a republic. They had committed a similar series of outrages in 1867. The present renewal of Fenian activity had begun in March of the previous year, 1883, with an explosion at the offices of *The Times* newspaper and the Local Government Office in Whitehall. These bombings, which involved extensive damage to several railway stations, including Paddington and Victoria, had continued to the present time, the explosions at Scotland Yard and St James's Square being merely the latest in the series of Fenian outrages. They were also seen as more serious than those of 1867, gunpowder having now been replaced by dynamite. This circumstance led to the virtual disappearance of the name *Fenian* and the more usual reference to these criminals as "The Dynamiters".

Despite the drafting into London of large numbers of extra police to guard public buildings – sixty-three at Buckingham Palace alone – the authorities had been singularly unsuccessful either in arresting any of the criminals or preventing a continuation of the bombings. For reasons which I did not fully understand, Sherlock Holmes was, for once, in complete agreement with Police Commissioner Henderson and Assistant Commissioner Monro, head of the CID, in thinking that his own talents were inappropriate to affording any help in the matter. But, only ten days before, Holmes' brother Mycroft had delivered a personal note from Harcourt, the Home Secretary. It was a request for Holmes' assistance – "from the highest authority in the land". It was, therefore, not a request which could be refused, even if it had been accepted by Holmes with the very greatest of reluctance.

....

A cab took Holmes and myself as far as Trafalgar Square. It appeared that half of London was bent upon reaching the same destination as ourselves – though with little success. So far as could be seen down both Whitehall and Northumberland Avenue, the roads were completely blocked by stationary traffic. Pedestrians were still more numerous, though it was obvious that were we to make any further progress, then it must be on foot.

The term "Scotland Yard" has become used almost universally, to describe the headquarters of the Metropolitan Police, and must, in the minds of many, be thought to be the name of a single building. Such is not the case. "Great Scotland Yard" is a place – a yard – all that now remains of what was once three yards named "Great", "Middle" and "Little". The last two have long been incorporated into what is now Whitehall Place. In 1820 some of the buildings in both Whitehall Place and Great Scotland Yard were taken over to house the headquarters of the Metropolitan Police. The fact that those headquarters are still housed in a number of buildings,

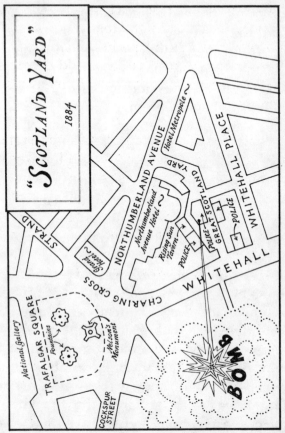

not all of them situated in Great Scotland Yard itself, but generally referred to as "Scotland Yard", is frequently a source of some public confusion.

It took some fifteen to twenty minutes to cover the short distance between a point in Trafalgar Square, close to Nelson's Monument, and the Whitehall entrance to Great Scotland Yard. By that time, the police had been forced to close off the Yard to the public, having found themselves unable to contain the very large numbers of would-be sightseers. That was a matter of considerable relief to Holmes and myself – if less so to others with business premises in the Yard. Not least of those was Mr Duncan, the landlord of the Rising Sun tavern who, though having been indisposed for several weeks, and having suffered numerous minor injuries from the explosion had, earlier that morning, been doing a brisk business with sightseers, whom he'd been charging threepence a head to view the damage to the barroom!

From the note which Holmes had received, and the constable's reference to the Rising Sun being "across the road", we had already concluded that the building which had received the damage was the one occupying the isolated position in the centre of the yard. It was an assumption almost instantly confirmed. When we caught sight of the building, it was all too apparent that the whole of the north-west corner had been blown away, leaving a gaping hole all of fifteen feet wide and nearly two storeys in height. Someone detached themselves from one of several groups of police in the yard and came towards us. I recognised the tall, flaxen-haired figure of Detective Sergeant Tobias Gregson. He greeted us in his usual, pleasant manner.

"They've the luck of the Devil, these bombers,"

Contemporary illustration of the bomb damage to Scotland Yard – From the Illustrated London News of June 7th 1884.

he said. "I don't believe they knew the exact location of Inspector Sweeny's office, any more than
that they'd calculated on their bomb bringing the
whole of a wall down. But you can be sure that it's
given them a deal of satisfaction – destroying the
office of a man only just appointed to assist in putting a stop to their infernal activities!"

"I can see four rooms exposed," Holmes
observed. "Sweeny's is one. Who occupied the
others?"

"Inspector MacDonald. One was a general
office, and the other's the Public Carriage Office."

"So," Holmes continued, "you and Lestrade
are among the more fortunate occupants of the
building."

"I wouldn't say that, Mr Holmes. You know
what the place was like before this happened.
Overcrowded offices, papers and files piled up on
the staircases. Everybody's going to have to move
around until the damage is repaired. I don't know
which I'd like least – having two more sharing that
impossibly small room with Lestrade and myself,
or moving out altogether. There's talk of some of
us having to go to King Street. And they tell me
that's worse than this was! But I'm sure that you
and Dr Watson aren't here to listen to my troubles.
I heard that your assistance had been sought, Mr
Holmes – but if it's Chief Inspector Littlechild you
were wanting to see, I can tell you that he's not
here."

"It's of no matter," Holmes assured him. "In

truth, Mr Gregson, I am not yet at all certain what kind of assistance I might be able to give. Since all of these explosions have taken place in public places, it is unlikely, for instance, that I am ever going to have the opportunity to make a full and detailed examination of the 'scene of the crime'."

That was the first precise reason Holmes had offered for what I already knew to be his reluctance to become involved in the investigation of these crimes. I did see the point that he was making. One had only to look at the mountain of wreckage strewn about the yard to realise that it could take many days to sift through all of it for possible clues. To close Great Scotland Yard completely for such a period of time was clearly unthinkable. Since all of the bombings were in public places, the obvious priority would always be to restore whatever services they provided, and as quickly as possible. Gregson's attention had been suddenly distracted by some movement across the yard.

"My chief inspector," he said, "looking this way and making signs at me. Perhaps he's about to tell me how many people are going to be sharing my office – or whether I still have one. I think, Mr Holmes, Dr Watson, that I shall have to leave you."

"Surely," Holmes answered. "My commiserations upon your problems. And perhaps you would also extend them, on my behalf, to Mr Lestrade."

"Thank you, Mr Holmes, and 'Yes', I will pass your commiserations on to Lestrade – though I'm not certain that he needs them. He is, after all, probably the only man in Scotland Yard who sees this bombing as something of a blessing in disguise!"

With that he walked off, hesitated, then turned momentarily back towards us. Obviously he had realised that we might be totally unaware of the reason for his surprising comment about Lestrade. He shouted to us across the yard. "Yesterday's *Telegraph* and *Graphic*. Look through the advertisements."

Gregson turned away for a second time, and was gone.

....

The morning was fine and warm, if spoilt by a blustery wind which met one on every corner. With precious little chance of securing an empty cab, we determined to walk back to Baker Street. We easily obtained a copy of *The Graphic* in Trafalgar Square, but it required a visit to no less than three shops before we were fortunate in obtaining a copy of the day before's *Telegraph*.

Our curiosity had been greatly raised by Gregson's cryptic remark about Lestrade, but the blustery wind precluded any idea of reading a newspaper on the street, and therefore the answer would have to wait until we returned to our lodgings. But, since Holmes had already raised with Gregson one reason for his reluctance to become involved with the bombings, I used this opportunity to question him further. Upon that matter, he showed no reluctance.

"In a nutshell, Watson," he said, "it's a question of logic. You know my methods. Give me a number of facts, and I will deduce their significance. That is possible because people and events tend to follow certain logical and therefore predictable patterns. But, in situations where the rules of logic are either changed or no longer observed, prediction becomes at best uncertain, at worst impossible.

"These bombings are very much a case in point. One is not dealing here with a single criminal mind, but with an extensive criminal organisation. Most certainly there are a small number of people in that organisation who make clear decisions of policy – like the bombing of railway stations. But I doubt whether those people are even to be found within the shores of this country. That part of the operation will be based in the United States of America or, as has recently been suspected, in one or more of the European capitals, most probably Paris. Those who carry out those policies *are* among us. There are many of them, but deliberately organised in small, largely independent units – so that the discovery of one in no way jeopardises the others. At this level, careful, logical planning is replaced by opportunism, indiscipline and, worst of all, by a blind fervour for the 'cause'. It is that which gives rise to what you may equally regard as boldness or foolishness. Whichever it is, it produces behaviour so totally unexpected, so totally unpredictable, that it defies all normal methods of preparedness or detection. What able criminal, intent upon blowing up Scotland Yard, would even contemplate the idea of openly walking up to it and merely depositing outside a large, heavy valise, with a bomb audibly ticking away inside it!"

Holmes had made his case very plain. But, in so doing, he seemed to be suggesting that there was simply no counter to the continuation of these outrages.

"I think, Watson, that there is not – nothing, that is, which would be publicly acceptable. I have no doubt that the present bombings will end. They will end when the perpetrators have made a sufficiency of mistakes – or sufficient of their number have been arrested through the assistance of informers. But there will never be an end to 'The Dynamiters', or their successors, so long as the 'cause' continues to exist. If it still exists a hundred years from now, be sure, Watson, that there will be those who still foolishly believe that the 'cause' can be furthered by such atrocities as we have witnessed today. Nothing will have changed, save possibly that their weapons of destruction will have become yet more powerful and even less discriminating against the lives of the innocent."

Chapter Two

The Engraver's Thumb

Sherlock Holmes was a man blessed with a deal more self discipline than I. My first thought on returning to Baker Street was to discover why Lestrade should, as Gregson had claimed, be "the only man in Scotland Yard who sees this bombing as something of a blessing in disguise". I had assumed that Holmes would share my eagerness – but I was wrong! Because of our visit to the Yard, the morning post, which still lay on the breakfast table, had received no more than a cursory glance. Nor had Holmes yet had the opportunity to read the personal and crime columns of *The Times*. Both, Holmes felt, took precedence over what he suggested would prove to be no more than yet another example of Detective Sergeant Lestrade's one outstanding ability – an astonishing aptitude for getting himself into either ridiculous or embarrassing situations! He was sure that I'd enjoy making the discovery for myself – and would doubtless take equal pleasure in acquainting him with it.

I had scanned the pages of both the *Graphic* and *Telegraph*, not once, but several times, yet without finding any reference in the advertisements, either to Lestrade, or to anything which might be connected with him. How long I'd spent in my search, I realised only when Holmes, having finished his own appointed tasks, enquired as to my progress – or perhaps, rather obviously, my complete lack of it! At his request, I handed him the *Telegraph*. He thumbed quite rapidly through its pages, very quickly handing me back the open newspaper with the words, "Page nine. The large advertisement at the bottom of the first two columns."

"Heavens!" I said. "I don't understand either how you could find it so quickly, Holmes, or how I could possibly have missed it – and so many times!"

"A classic case of the pea and the elephant," Holmes replied. "Start with the assumption that the object for which you search is of the order of size of a pea and you'll most certainly ignore anything as large as an elephant. Your failure to find anything, suggested that to be the reason. So you see, Watson, I looked only at the elephants! I have but glanced at the advertisement and after all your hard work, I'm sure you deserve to be the first to read it in full. Perhaps if you would be so good as to read it aloud, then we can enjoy it together."

The advertisement was headed *WILSON'S FAMOUS TRAINED CANARIES*, and below, in slightly smaller type, were the words, *AS RECOMMENDED BY SCOTLAND YARD*. That surprising announcement was followed by no less surprising an explanation:

WILSON'S CANARIES, trained by the secret methods known, hitherto, only to the peasants of Germany's Harz Mountains, already provide a lasting pleasure in many of London's more gracious homes. Their exceptionally varied and unrivalled song has proved itself a delight to all who own them, and the envy of those who do not.

Such is the excellence of a WILSON CANARY that one could not expect of them, any greater reward than their beautiful singing already provides. So it is with some astonishment that we are excited to announce a truly amazing discovery. The ownership of a WILSON CANARY may also protect your home from burglarious entry!

We are reliably informed that several would-be thieves have recently been thwarted in their criminal intent, the household having been awakened to the presence of the intruder by a shrill and timely alarm given by a WILSON CANARY!

We could offer no more reliable testimony than that of Detective Sergeant Godfrey Lestrade of Scotland Yard, who has stated, "There is no denying that it was the birds that frightened off the intruders. I can see these canaries putting watch dogs out of business."

I paused. I suppose that I might have found myself laughing, but my immediate feeling was rather one of disbelief that even Lestrade could have allowed himself to be party to such indiscretion.

"Believe it, Watson," Holmes said, with his usual unnerving habit of answering unasked questions! "Have no doubt that he said it – though I'm sure in circumstances where he had no inkling of the use which might be made of his answer. As you're aware, Watson, I do hold Lestrade in small regard, but I bear no malice towards the man. I would hope that he is right in supposing that last evening's events will serve to divert attention from his latest unwitting stupidity. Yet, that apart, I do find myself not a little intrigued by the idea of canary burglar alarms – though I must confess I have never heard of 'Wilson's Famous Trained Canaries'. What else does this advertisement tell us?"

The answer was virtually nothing that added significantly to what I had already read aloud – except that "Archibold Wilson's Emporium of Singing Birds" was located in Bishopsgate Street Without, close to Liverpool Street Railway Station.

Holmes was silent for several moments.

"I'm sorry, Watson," he said, at last. My mind was on the name Archibold Wilson. I have reason to remember a man known as 'Artful Archie Wilson', though I'd not associate him with anything so pleasant as canaries! I suppose that it is a combination of names common enough."

Having found the corresponding advertisement in the *Graphic*, and satisfied myself that it was the same, I ventured to ask Holmes what plans he might have for the rest of the day.

"None, Watson, except to pursue in my mind that same matter which has been preoccupying it for these last ten days – these so-called 'Dynamiters and my obligation to be seen to make some contribution, at least to shorten, if not to stop the present series of bomb outrages. From what I told you this morning during our walk back from Scotland Yard, I'm sure that you appreciate the difficulty of that task. What I most fear is its impossibility!"

"If I can help . . ." I said. "I do know that if you are at a loss, Holmes, then my own talents are almost certainly useless – but the wish is sincere."

"And sincerely appreciated, Watson. I regret, my friend, that you can do no more than continue to tolerate my periods of mental detachment and consequent unsociability. But you aren't obliged to sit and watch them! It's a not unpleasant day. I'm sure you can find some better way of occupying your time than spending it in silence within these four walls."

....

Taking Holmes' advice, I spent much of the afternoon in the relaxed and pleasant surroundings of the Regent's Park Zoological Gardens. Returning to Baker Street in good time for our evening meal, my expectation was to find Holmes curled up, catlike, in a chair and the air blue with tobacco smoke. Possible alternatives would have been that he was lying upon his bed, contemplating the ceiling, or that he was scraping at his violin with an indifference which considerably belied his true skill. It was, in fact, none of these. I found him sitting at the table, apparently making copious notes from a slim volume which lay open beside him. As I entered the room, he plunged his hand beneath the sheets of paper that surrounded him, and withdrew a second, larger, book which he held out towards me. "Tell me, Watson," he asked. "What memories does that recall?"

The book was a collection of engravings by the artist, Thomas Bewick. I recalled that my father had several Bewick prints on the wall of his study. "Mostly cows", was my recollection.

Holmes clearly found that funny!

"That," he said, "must be quite the greatest understatement of the man's very remarkable talents as an illustrator of British wildlife. I'm not, as you know Watson, a great admirer of art, but Bewick has appealed to me since I was a child – if less for the artistic effect than the man's extra-ordinary powers of observation of detail. Open the book at the 'Foreword' and look at the small embellishment on the page opposite."

"It's obviously a print made from the end of a finger dipped in ink. Is that in some way remark-able?"

"Yes, Watson. First, because it is not made, as

you say, from a finger dipped in ink. It's an engraving which Bewick made of his own thumb. Second, because the pattern of lines on the engraver's thumb is as unique to its late owner as was his signature."

I'd heard this said of the pattern of lines on the fingers – though I was becoming a little confused. What connection had it with the Bewick prints in my father's study!

"None, Watson. I was not even aware that your father *was* the possessor of some Bewick prints. All that I had expected of my question, was that the book would bring back memories of our visit to Hay on Wye."

It should have! We had visited Hay less than a year before, and in circumstances where my memories of it *should* have remained most vivid (The Case of the Howling Dog). But I *had* forgotten – until now.

"You bought it at that book auction in Hay. You bought two books. I remember thinking the other one a rather unlikely choice – written in Latin and by someone with an equally unlikely name – Popinjay?"

"Not bad, Watson. The name is *Purkenje*, and the book is a printed version of a Latin thesis on finger impressions, originally delivered as a lecture at the University of Breslau in 1823. I did buy it partly out of interest, but more so in the knowledge that it is an exceptionally rare book offered at a ridiculously low price. In truth Watson, I had myself forgotten about both books. Indeed it was only having come upon Bewick by accident, and seeing the print of the engraver's thumb, that I was reminded of Purkenje. And, as you see, I've not only found Purkenje but, thanks to the painfully thorough grounding in Latin which I suffered at Winchester, I've almost completed the translation."

"And you are hoping," I suggested, "that this will prove to be of some assistance in your investigation of these bombings."

"Oh no, Watson! Call it rather a piece of therapy. When my mind becomes so set upon a problem, in which clearly I am making no progress, I find it sometimes helps to break my fixed patterns of thought by embarking upon some other quite unrelated problem. And I have long promised myself the opportunity to consider the merits of finger impressions as compared with the Bertillon system."

I admitted to knowing very little about either.

"Then let me explain. You know my oft expressed opinions upon the value of having a central registry of criminal records. And an essential feature of such a registry is that it provides a means of positively identifying known criminals, no matter how much they might have attempted to change their appearance. The French police have operated such a registry for three years, using for purposes of identification, a system devised by Alphonse Bertillon. The Bertillon system relies upon taking a large number of physical measurements of the bony parts of the body. It is a most cumbersome method, though it does appear to work. Finger impressions or 'prints', have long suggested themselves as a simpler alternative – because they rely upon just one single physical characteristic. The pattern of ridges on the fingers is unique to each individual and remains unaltered by age or disease."

"Which would surely appear to make it the simpler method," I observed.

"It would," Holmes answered, "but for one thing. Here – take my magnifying glass and look at the ends of your own fingers, Watson. Look at the complex pattern of ridges. To say that two such patterns are identical, one must do more than merely look at their general appearance. One must first devise a simple and reliable means by which they can be classified. No system has yet been devised which is both simple enough *and* reliable enough to satisfy the police force of any western nation. For centuries, China has used thumb prints on seals of contract. And even now, Sir Edward Henry, the Commissioner of Police in Bengal is working on what he believes may prove to be a practical solution."

"What about Purkenje?" I asked.

"Too complicated," Holmes replied, "though I do already see ways in which it might be simplified. But I must first finish the translation."

I left Holmes to his work, intending that he

should remain uninterrupted, at least until the arrival of our evening meal, but that was not to be. Only fifteen minutes later there was a knock on the street door. Being near to the window, I pressed my face to the glass in an attempt to see who it might be, though without success. As I turned from the window I noticed Holmes observing me with quite the oddest of expressions. But this did not seem to be the time for explanations. Footsteps on the stairs already suggested that we were to have a second visitor that day and, it transpired, a most unexpected one. It was Lestrade!

....

Through his narrow face and sallowness of skin often disguised our visitor's true emotions, Lestrade did, on this occasion, look distinctly uncomfortable. Holmes could adopt a quite sphinx-like expression, but I wondered whether my own face displayed anything of the embarrassment I was feeling. Lestrade refused the offer of a seat, saying that he'd come only to deliver a message. One of the bombs placed in St James's Square had failed to explode. It was still complete, packed in its valise and untouched except for the removal of its detonators. It had been transferred to the Royal Arsenal at Woolwich where it would be dismantled in the morning by one of the Arsenal's explosives experts. Because of Holmes' recent official involvement, Inspector Littlechild had wondered if he might wish to be present at the dismantling.

"The necessity," Lestrade said, "for my presence here, and not someone more junior, is that I carry a written authority, signed by Assistant Commissioner Monro, allowing your entry into the Arsenal, Mr Holmes. Security at the Arsenal is always strict, but has had to become much more so because of these bombings. I'm afraid, Dr Watson, that the written authority does not include yourself."

I said that I quite understood. Lestrade was about to leave us when Holmes, this time himself showing some sign of hesitancy, said, "It seems a little ridiculous, Mr Lestrade, that you should leave us without knowing the answer to the question which is so clearly troubling you. 'Yes', Dr Watson and myself do know about these unfortunate advertisements. I'm sure that even if you did say the words attributed to you, you did not say them in your official capacity, nor had you any idea that they might be used in this way. It's nothing short of a criminal deceit, but of a kind where you have little chance of obtaining redress – not without the very real risk of exposing yourself to even worse publicity. I want only to say that you have my sympathy and, I'm sure, that of Dr Watson."

If Lestrade's mouth did not actually open, it's certain that his jaw dropped ever so slightly. I both understood and shared his surprise. Holmes' usual conversations with Lestrade might best be described as "verbal fencing". I could recall no previous occasion upon which Holmes had uttered a single kindly word to the man! Lestrade did find his tongue.

"Thank you, Mr Holmes. Thank you very much. I'll tell you that yours are the very first words of either understanding or sympathy which I've yet received. And, may I say that you have, with your usual astuteness, stated the exact truth of the matter. The conversation in fact took place in the bar-room of the Rising Sun, with a man who said he worked for *The Times*. He asked about these several recent cases where burglars had been scared off by canaries. I'd heard of none of them, but then I wouldn't. If unsuccessful break-ins are reported at all, then it's to the local police, and not Scotland Yard. And not much is done about them. All I said was, 'If it's true, then it seems there's no denying it was the birds that frightened off the intruders.' The other bit was a parting joke, or so I thought. I said, 'If we get enough cases like that, then I can see these canaries putting watch dogs out of business'."

"You said you'd heard of none of these cases?"

"I hadn't, Mr Holmes, though you can guess that I've since made some discreet enquiries. It does seem that it's true – four reported in the last two months, and all in A Division. I suppose I should see that as a small consolation!"

Having renewed his gratitude, Lestrade insisted that he must leave. When he'd gone, Holmes stood, for some time, just staring towards the window, and then, turning to me, said, "Yes, Watson. It could prove to be most interesting."

"Your visit to the Arsenal," I hazarded.

"Surely that will – though it wasn't what I'd most immediately in mind. Before Lestrade's arrival, you were standing at the window, with your face and hand on the glass. Do you remember where you placed your hand?"

I thought I did.

"Then take my magnifying glass, return to the window, breathe on the spot where you placed your hand and, using the glass, tell me what you see."

I did as Holmes bid me.

"There's an impression on the glass – of a part of my hand and the tips of my fingers!" I told him. "It is barely visible, since it's there only for an instant unless, of course, I keep breathing on the glass."

"Just so, Watson, but suppose that there were some way in which those impressions could be 'fixed' – some way of making them clearly visible for long enough to photograph them!"

Chapter Three

The Last of the Kidsmen

The following day was Sunday. With few early morning trains running from Cannon Street Station to Woolwich, Holmes had left Baker Street before I was awake. He returned in time for a late lunch which Mrs Hudson had held back with something less than her usual good grace, declaring that her Sunday roast would be well and truly ruined – again!

It was! But that was never the kind of matter upon which Holmes was likely to pass comment, especially when he regarded the food which he was eating as no more than a necessary, but tiresome interruption to the smooth flow of conversation. In this case it was not so much a "conversation", as a lecture – by Holmes.

Holmes had returned from the Arsenal at Woolwich, clearly excited. There were, apparently, two reasons – in some way connected. The first, was what he'd seen there. The second was an idea that he'd been developing in his mind during last evening – and probably during most of the night. If it were possible to "fix" and identify the finger prints of anyone who had handled an object then, potentially, it offered a revolutionary new technique in the investigation of crime. He did attempt to explain to me the connection between that idea and his visit to the Arsenal.

My failure to understand most of it, may have been partly due to Holmes giving his explanation between mouthfuls of slightly burned roast beef, dried up cabbage and overboiled potatoes, but he did leave me with a general, if perhaps not entirely accurate, impression of his argument.

If it were possible to "fix" and "identify" the finger prints which might be found upon bombs that had failed to explode, or even upon parts of bombs that had exploded, then it could provide a means of building up a picture of the people who'd handled them. Specifically, it might answer certain questions. Did the firing mechanisms arrive assembled? How many people packed the dynamite into the valises? Did those who did the packing, also place the bombs at their targets?

I was not certain that I saw the value of such information unless the finger prints could be matched with actual people, but I had no doubt that it was something of which Holmes must be aware. In any case, he was still going on!

"I have to say, Watson, that no one at the

Arsenal this morning shared my enthusiasm. I admit that I could have made a better case if I'd already devised a means of 'fixing' finger prints on objects. I have, at least, been given the under-taking that, from now on, none of the potential bomb 'evidence' will be handled more than is absolutely necessary. The Arsenal will give me every co-operation possible, and I have been promised the use of the photographic equipment at Scotland Yard. I fear, Watson, that for the near future, I may be frequently missing from Baker Street – and when I *am* here, I could well be too busy to be good company."

....

Holmes had not been "good company" for many days already and, even if the reason had now changed, the effect was the same. It was a situation to which I was well used and I did not have much difficulty in occupying my time. Inevitably, one of those occupations was reading, and I will confess to giving more than my usual attention to those newspapers and magazines most likely to have made some comment upon Lestrade's latest indiscretion. The police were the constant butt of press criticism, often of the most unfair and scurrilous kind. The fact that I discovered nothing was, therefore, a matter of some astonishment. It did appear that Lestrade's best hopes about the distraction of the bombing had been fulfilled!

Nearly two weeks later, and Holmes still totally preoccupied with his task, Lestrade would have passed completely from my mind but for the appearance of yet another series of advertisements for Wilson's Canaries. They were not the same as the first, but rather a sequel to them, their purpose being best explained in the opening words of the advertisements themselves:

Following upon the recent discovery that a WILSON CANARY is not merely a songbird of unrivalled quality, but a proven protection against burglarious entry to the home, we have been gratified by the unprecedented degree of public interest which has been shown.

We are, therefore, especially delighted to be able to announce the availability – to both present and intending owners of a WILSON CANARY – of the new and exclusively designed WILSON AUDIOPHONIC CANARY CAGE.

This cage, whilst sacrificing nothing of the elegance expected by clients, now incorporates a system of sound magnification based upon the latest and most advanced scientific knowledge of audiophonics. Fully adjustable, the WILSON AUDIOPHONIC CANARY CAGE will not merely enhance the volume of beautiful birdsong but now provides an alarm against night intruders guaranteed to awaken even the most heavy of sleepers.

No mention was made of either Lestrade or Scotland Yard. There were just the words "officially approved by the authorities". There was also a diagram which purported to illustrate the "audiophonic principles" upon which the cage worked. Feeling that my own knowledge of the physical

The *"Wilson Audiophonic Canary Cage"* – an illustration taken from a contemporary advertisement.

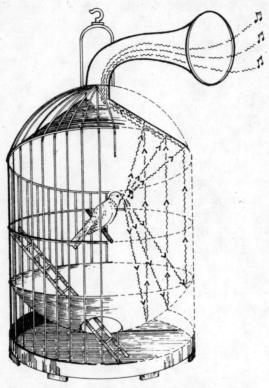

sciences was not such that I could make any reliable judgement as to the practicality of the device, I decided to show it to Holmes.

That seemingly simple decision proved more difficult to accomplish than could be imagined by anyone who had not experienced Sherlock Holmes in one of his periods of more feverish activity. As he had warned, he was frequently absent from our lodgings, though he did spend many hours at Baker Street each day. But always, it seemed, he was working – even in the middle of the night! I neither knew, nor would I have understood, the precise nature of his research. It was all to do with the "fixing" of finger prints and, to that end, he was experimenting with the effects of various powders, solutions and vapours.

That much, I learned – if "indirectly". I had on several occasions been sent on errands to Meacher, Higgins and Thomas, the chemists in Crawford Street, almost around the corner. There I'd purchased an astonishing variety of powders, from jeweller's rouge to ladies' face powder – Mrs Hudson having complained that Holmes had used her entire stock of the latter. The number of solutions in use could be gauged from the fact that Holmes, having taken to eating while he worked, appeared rarely to return his cups – pressing them into service to supplement his dwindling stock of chemical glassware. The use of various vapours was more self-evident – sometimes at the moment of entering the premises from the street door!

I relate all this only by way of explaining why it took me thirty-six hours to succeed in persuading Holmes even to glance at the advertisement which I had already tried a dozen times to bring to his attention. In the circumstances, the mild admonition that I really should have shown it to him as soon as I'd seen it, seemed best ignored. I said that I'd merely hoped to have his opinion on whether such a device could work. I did not feel qualified to make a judgement.

"Nor I," was Holmes reply. "That I am sure can be remedied, though it may be of no importance. Watson – you see that I am busy. You did offer your help."

I did, and thought I had been giving it, both in running errands, and in pacifying Mrs Hudson – though apparently Holmes discounted such trivia.

"I have a problem," Holmes continued.

I said that I had noticed it!

"No, Watson. I'm not referring to my work on finger prints. That is going well, though there is still much work to be done. The problem to which I refer is that we now have another case. It could not have occurred at a more inconvenient time, especially as I attach a deal of importance to it."

I certainly wasn't aware of any new case, though I was already prepared to accept its importance. For the first time in two weeks, Holmes had actually left his experiments and settled himself in his favourite chair – with the apparent intention of talking to me!

"Tell me, Watson," he asked. "Have you ever heard the term, 'kidsman'?"

I could not recall it.

"But you are an admirer of the writings of Mr Charles Dickens, and I therefore imagine that you have read *Oliver Twist* and that you remember the character, *Fagin*."

I had, and I did.

"Fagin was a 'kidsman', a manager of child thieves. Such men were commonplace in the 'nethersheken' – the low-down lodging houses of Dickens' London. Fagin is a character who is remarkably true to life, even to his methods of training his child pickpockets. There is one omission. An added incentive to their learning was the frequent use of beatings, kicking and starvation!"

"But" I said, "these children weren't prisoners. Why did they tolerate such treatment?"

"It was very simply the least of several evils, Watson. Such children could starve on the streets, or be given 'a place of occupation' in the care of the poor law authorities – a fate regarded with more dread than a spell in gaol! But let me not wander too far from the point of what I tell you. At the time when you and I were still at school, in the sixties, the kidsmen were a vanishing class of criminal. Not, I may say, because of the improvements in social conditions or effectiveness of the law. The demise of the kidsman was brought about by nothing more dramatic than a change in fashion. For men, it was the disappearance of the tail coat with a pocket in the tail which usually contained a large silk handkerchief. Snuff-taking declined, and with it the snuff box. For the ladies who carried a purse in the pocket of their skirts, a change in design of the skirt that brought the front, containing the pocket, close to the body, meant that the purse could no longer be removed with impunity. Picking of pockets, of course, continues, but now demands a much greater degree of skill and teamwork than can reasonably be accomplished by children."

"So," I said, "the kidsmen have disappeared."

"The answer to that, Watson, is 'almost'. Some turned to other forms of crime. A few became honest citizens. A very few sought other ways of employing children to further their criminal activities. One such was a man generally known as 'Artful Archie Wilson'."

I had at last seen some point to what Holmes had been telling me. The name 'Archie Wilson' had been mentioned at the time when Holmes and I had first seen the advertisements for 'Wilson's Famous Trained Canaries'. Holmes had wondered whether Archie Wilson and Archibold Wilson could be one and the same.

"They are, Watson. You know that I've been spending a deal of my time at Scotland Yard – and there are still some at the Yard who not only have good reason to remember Wilson, but also to make it their business to keep a watchful eye on anything he might be doing."

"Like training and selling canaries?" I queried.

"If that were all I thought he was doing," Holmes answered, "we would not be holding this conversation. Let me tell you what I know of the man. And let me first surprise you by telling you that I have never, in fact, met or even seen him. Go back to the time when I came down from Oxford, determined upon becoming a consulting detective and conscious of a need greatly to improve my knowledge of crime and criminals. As a part of that education, I got to know my London. More especially I got to know the places and the people that make up its vast, criminal underworld. It was then that I first heard of Archie Wilson. You must understand, Watson, that even among criminals, there are carefully defined social strata – a *macer* and a *magsman* are both cheats and card sharps, but the *macer*, being the more skilful, looks upon the *magsman* as his inferior. Archie Wilson, it seemed, was looked upon as everybody's inferior! It wasn't because of his lack of ability – the man had a certain perverted genius. It was his methods – a ruthless exploitation of children, sickening even to those whom you, Watson, might think little better!

"I never saw the man, because he had at that time, recently 'gone to earth'. It was common gossip that over the years, more of 'Wilson's children' had died of starvation and beatings than had ever reached manhood. Now, at last, he'd been brought to court on a charge of double murder – a boy aged eight, and his brother, a five-year old. But the case was dismissed through lack of evidence. The witnesses, mostly children, had either disappeared, or changed their evidence. Wilson had gone to earth because it seemed very likely that the criminal fraternity were about to do to him what the law had regrettably failed to do!

"In those days, Watson, I saw myself as a

crusader against crime and criminals, especially
that kind of criminal which I held in lowest regard
– those who are a danger to society, those who are
ruthless or greedy, and, not least, those who
mercilessly exploit the weakest and most vulner-
able members of our society, the young, the old
and the poor. I fear that my crusader's armour
may have become much tarnished with the passing of the years, but one thing stays bright in my
memory. I saw such men as Wilson as the very
antithesis of everything which I held to be good
and decent. I promised myself that, given the
opportunity, I would spare no effort to remove
such cankers from the face of society. I could not
have foreseen that when that opportunity did come,
it would be none other than Wilson himself!"

I knew Holmes to be a man of high principle,
and I could share his feelings of disgust. Equally, I
could see his dilemma. If he was right in his
assumption that Wilson *was* engaged in criminal
activity, then this was an opportunity which he'd
long awaited – a matter almost of honour. Yet
Holmes was already stretched to the utmost of his
mental and physical resources with his assign-
ment at Scotland Yard. I saw no way in which he
could devote time to yet another investigation.

"And the fact is, Watson, that I cannot. But all
may not be lost! You offered your help. I wish to
accept your offer. You must do for me what I cannot. You must investigate the Wilson case!"

It was a suggestion for which I found myself to

be totally unprepared. In the three years that I had spent with Holmes, three years in which I had observed and, I believed, learned much of his methods, I had increasingly felt a little slighted that Holmes had not begun to entrust me with some of his more demanding work. I now felt that I had indeed been "hoist with my own petard"! It was no consolation to observe that Holmes was watching my reactions with a broad, almost childish grin on his face!

"You look quite alarmed, Watson. You have no need. I would not ask the impossible of you. I ask only that you will lend me your eyes and ears. You will still have the use of my mind to do the rest."

Holmes did not wait for my answer before removing his watch from his pocket.

"I must leave you. I am expected at the Yard in fifteen minutes – to see the results of the photographic work which they have been doing for me. We will talk again."

Holmes was already preparing to leave, but I seized upon the opportunity to ask one question.

"You said that it was through your friends at the Yard that you'd discovered Archie Wilson and Archibold Wilson to be the same man. You also implied that he was engaged in something criminal. I assume that you also know what?"

"No Watson. I do not know what. Nor did anyone at the Yard tell me that Wilson was up to anything unusual. You did – when you showed me that latest advertisement."

Chapter Four

The Case of the Silent Canary

Whatever time it was when Holmes returned from Scotland Yard, it was after I was in bed and asleep. He had left the house again next morning before I was up. Indeed the only evidence that he had been home at all was a note, left for me on the breakfast table. It read, "My Dear Watson, since the Wilson case is yours, I would not want you to feel that I was interfering unduly, even before you have had an opportunity to begin! However, as I assume that it is your intention to visit the Emporium in Bishopsgate this morning, I can foresee one small problem which, doubtless, has already exercised your mind and in which I may be of some small assistance. Obviously you have decided to present yourself as a potential customer, concerned about the protection of your not inconsiderable valuables – therefore considerably interested in the advertisements, though not unnaturally, sceptical of their worth. The problem which I foresee is that while, clearly, you will use a fictitious name, you may also need an address – other than Baker Street. It is in that matter where I can assist. Under the blotter on my desk you will find the private visiting card of my tailor, Mr Smallbone. I'll not insult your intelligence by explaining the reason why, being sure that you will already have seen the wisdom of neither giving your address, nor presenting the card until you feel that you are nearing the end of your conversation with Mr Wilson."

"Well done!" I said, aloud.

"Not more so than usual, Dr Watson."

I had failed to notice that Mrs Hudson had entered the room with a tray of toast and coffee.

"Not the toast, Mrs Hudson," I assured her. "That is always done to perfection. I was referring to this note from Mr Holmes."

She left, but not before gathering up three cups from where Holmes had been working on his experiments!

I read the note again, over my toast and coffee. I had to give Holmes full marks for ingenuity, if not for subtlety. He had left me full and exact instructions upon what he required me to do, but couched in a manner that, were I to accuse him of it, I would be met with feigned hurt and disappointment that I should even have thought him capable of it!

I would have been happier had I understood

why the advertisement which I had shown to Holmes only the day before, had so immediately convinced him that Wilson was up to no good. It clearly had some connection with the so-called "audiophonic cage" – though I failed to see what! Holmes had admitted to sharing my own ignorance as to whether the scientific principle upon which it was claimed to work, was a sound one. He had even suggested that that might be of no consequence. Nor had I had any single inspiration upon the matter when, later that morning, I set off by cab for Bishopsgate Street Without.

I cannot say that my first impressions of "Archibold Wilson's Emporium of Singing Birds" were entirely surprising since, in truth, I had no real preconception of it. My last recollection of caged birds was from the days of my youth when, it may be unusually, those few which could be bought in my home town were stocked in plain, wire-fronted boxes by the local ironmonger! I was certain that there would be no similarities, as indeed there were not.

A large, double-fronted shop was bedecked over the whole of its exterior with an astonishing number and variety of cages, many designed in imitation of pagodas, temples, or Swiss chalets – or recognisable as replicas in miniature of such buildings as St Paul's and even the Crystal Palace of the Great Exhibition! Of the occupants of these remarkable cages, it must be said that while their concerted singing was not always melodious, its

Perhaps not surprisingly, no photograph can be found of Wilson's Emporium of Singing Birds. Some indication of its appearance may, however, be gathered from this photograph, taken in 1880, of Palmer's Pet Store in nearby Sclater Street.

volume was such as to rise over both the steady street noise and the intermittent, yet more strident sounds, of the nearby Great Eastern Railway.

Archibold Wilson was, I might say, at least by contrast with the flamboyance of his wares unusually commonplace. He was a small man, slightly built, neatly dressed, bespectacled and with white hair receding from his temples. He was quietly well spoken, and in every way pleasantly helpful in response to my enquiries.

....

"Which, you found surprising," Holmes remarked, "especially after my account of Archibold Wilson's past history. But then, Watson, I've never subscribed to Lauvergne's or Lombroso's theories of the existence of 'the criminal type'. A man's true character may be in no way reflected in either his appearance or manner."

Holmes had returned to Baker Street that same afternoon, armed with a number of photographs of finger prints. He had immediately seated himself by the window and proceeded to examine them with his magnifying glass, though assuring me that that need not prevent my recounting the events of my morning's visit to Bishopsgate.

"You, of course asked about the cage," he prompted.

"Naturally," I replied, "and I was given a demonstration of one being assembled."

"Assembled"?

"I was about to explain. The amplifying

mechanism requires exact adjustment, which may easily be upset during transportation. The parts are, therefore, stored in a large wooden crate and would normally be assembled in the actual room of the house where the customer required it."

"And who carried the crate from the back premises into the shop?"

"How did you know –"

"A trifle, Watson. The shop is clearly intended to be of elegant appearance, not a place for storing wooden crates. It had, therefore, to be brought in. You described Wilson as 'small' and 'slight' and the crate as 'large'. So he needed assistance. I'm merely asking 'Who carried, or helped to carry it?'"

"Two young boys," I told him.

"So the crate was large, but light."

I supposed it must have been. The boys were both small – one hardly bigger than the crate!

"Twenty-three," Holmes suddenly announced.

"Twenty-three?"

"I'm sorry, Watson. I was counting the ridges on this print from the centre of the pattern to the point at which the pattern breaks. But do please continue."

I related how Mr Wilson had unpacked and assembled the parts of the cage "though," I added, "he was unable to give me an actual demonstration of the amplifying effect of the system. He explained that were he then to place a canary in the cage, the strangeness of its surroundings would most certainly discourage its singing for some time. I thought that not unreasonable. And I will tell you this, Holmes. If it was in your mind that it was Wilson's intention to foist some useless, yet expensive device, upon a gullible public, that would not appear to be the case. My impression was that his prices were exceptionally reasonable."

"You do frequently astonish me, Watson! I would not have expected you to be so knowledgeable upon the price of bird cages!"

I did not tell Holmes that I was not! On leaving the shop, I had hailed a cab and asked the driver if he knew of any similar establishment. He had taken me to Palmer's in Sclater Street, half a mile distant. A comparison with Palmer's prices had shown Wilson to be the cheaper, especially his "audiophonic cage", for which he was asking what I thought to be an almost ridiculously modest sum. Holmes did not pursue the point. Instead, he asked what had happened at the moment at which I had produced Mr Smallbone's card.

That *had* surprised me. On presenting the card, I had sensed a sudden change in attitude on Wilson's part. It was, admittedly, no more than an impression, but I did have the strong feeling that he was suddenly no longer interested in my custom. It was not the name, "Smallbone" – I had given that shortly after entering the shop – yet

"Bow Street" was a perfectly respectable address.

"Ah!" Holmes observed. "I did tell you that Mr Wilson had 'gone to earth' after the murder trial, I assume in some place well outside London. That was some years ago. Perhaps he still remembers Bow Street for the reputation which it may still have enjoyed at the time of his leaving."

"Which was?" I queried.

"As the location of a number of somewhat disreputable brothels, though I assure you, Watson, they are long gone and the street is, as you say, now perfectly respectable. Perhaps it shows Mr Wilson in a new light – that he is really particular about the suitability of potential homes for his 'famous singing canaries'!"

Holmes was, of course, joking – though I did not find it funny that my custom might have been rejected, and by such a person as Wilson, because he had identified me as a brothel-keeper! The fact that Holmes made no attempt to disguise his own amusement at the idea seemed only to worsen my feelings of affront.

"I'm truly sorry, Watson. That thought had not occurred to me when I left you the visiting card. But don't let that misfortune detract from the fact that you have made an excellent beginning."

I failed to see that I had done anything worthwhile. It seemed to me that Holmes could be wrong in supposing that Wilson was engaged in anything other than promoting a doubtful product by dishonest means. There seemed to have been such a general lowering of standards of honesty in advertising of recent years, I wouldn't have thought Wilson exceptional. I was only curious to know what Holmes expected me to do next.

"I, Watson? The case is yours! Indeed, I would seem to have caused you such upset by my small but well intentioned gesture of assistance, I do promise to leave the matter entirely in your own capable hands."

Holmes clearly imagined that I had so far failed to see his subterfuge. I had as yet done nothing of my own volition, merely carried out the instructions which *he* had provided in his note. Two could play at that game! I resolved to do nothing, but wait – wait to see what device he would use to provide me with my next set of instructions, as I knew he surely would!

....

Nothing happened for something like two weeks – except for what might be regarded as a slight weakening in my own resolution. Being in Long Acre on a matter of personal business, I visited Bow Street, to assure myself of the truth of what Holmes had said of it. He was clearly right. It *was* a respectable street. Indeed, Mr Smallbone's lodging was not merely opposite the Royal Italian Opera Company and Floral Hall, but literally next door to the Police Station and Magistrates Court! My other weakening was to buy two books on canaries – Wallace's *Canary Book*, and a reprinted and "much revised" version of Blagrove's *Epitome of Husbandry*, first published as long ago as 1675 but, I'd discovered, containing most of the so called "secrets" of the peasants of the Harz Mountains!

I have no doubt that any account which I might give of those secrets, must do less than justice to what is, in reality, a matter of great skill and patience, though the principles at least, I did not find too difficult to understand. Canaries are, in fact, trained in their singing, much as are human opera singers, their tutors varying from nightingales to "bird organs" – ingenious mechanical devices which exactly imitate the natural song. And whilst, hitherto, I might have described the song of the canary as "pleasant", I was to learn that the accomplished bird can produce no less than thirteen distinct song passages, each named in such imaginative terms as the "bell roll" or the "deep bubbling water tour"!

In St Andreasberg, in the centre of the Harz region, competitions are held to determine the finest singing birds. To ensure that the birds will sing at the moment required, advantage is taken of the bird's natural instinct to waken and join in the "dawn chorus". The bird is kept in a darkened cage, so that it imagines it to be night – until a door is opened, letting in the light. The bird, now supposing it to be dawn, will then promptly oblige with its full singing repertoire, or so it is hoped!

Holmes had, for some mornings past, actually

breakfasted with me at the normal hour, even finding time for some conversation before his inevitable departure, either to Scotland Yard or the Arsenal at Woolwich. The conversation, rather one-sided and not always entirely intelligible to me, was inevitably upon the subject of finger prints and the progress which he was making. That morning, I had been greatly tempted to change the topic – and at the same time, display what I now considered to be my extensive knowledge on the subject of canaries. I'd resisted that temptation, with difficulty, feeling that it might be misinterpreted as a hint of my failure to think of any really constructive way of pursuing the "Wilson Case". Apart from my continuing conviction that there was no "case" to pursue, I had still not entirely forgiven Holmes for the last trick which he had played upon me.

Holmes was about to depart, and checking the contents of an attaché case when, with what might have been a grunt of annoyance, he produced and handed to me a copy of the satirical publication, *Judy*.

"I had really meant to give it to you last night," he said. "I have turned down the corner of the relevant page. I shall be late, Watson – possibly very late. Mrs Hudson can certainly assume that I shall not be here for an evening meal."

With that, he left me.

....

The "relevant" page was headed, "The Case of

the Silent Canary". Readers may already have guessed, as I did myself upon seeing that title, something of the content of what lay below it. At a little before midnight on the previous Monday, a successful robbery had taken place at a house in Carlton House Terrace. Numerous small items, some of very considerable value, had been removed from a first floor room where, on that very same morning, a Wilson Canary had been installed, complete with audiophonic cage. Far from alerting the household, the canary had apparently remained silent.

The writer of the piece might, most fairly, have focussed criticism upon what were, demonstrably, the exaggerated claims made in the recent advertisements. Instead, I suppose in keeping with the editorial policy of that particular publication, it had been shamelessly used for yet another attack upon the police in general and, inevitably, upon Detective Sergeant Lestrade in particular.

Though I had no more regard for Lestrade as a policeman than did Holmes, my immediate reaction was to feel incensed at so obvious an injustice. Many *were* beginning to feel that writers in newspapers and periodicals too often abused their freedom, particularly at the expense of individuals with no opportunity to reply. It was, undoubtedly, my preoccupation with those thoughts which considerably delayed my realisation that this article might have other significance!

Was the fact that I had been given the article just

The Case of the Silent Canary

A cartoon which appeared in Judy in the week following the publication of the article. Whilst clearly inspired by the article, it refers also to a heated argument of that time as to whether policemen should be issued with whistles or rattles. The caricatures are of Police Commissioner Henderson (left) and Assistant Commissioner Monro of the CID.

*Didn't I always say that a rattle was
more reliable than a whistle?*

as Holmes was leaving, genuinely the oversight that he claimed it to be? Was the presence of the canary and its unfortunate silence during the robbery only what it appeared, or was it the very kind of development that Holmes had been expecting all along? Was this, indeed, intended to represent my "next set of instructions" for which I had so long been waiting? If it was, then Holmes was going to be disappointed. Either I was wrong or, this time, he was being altogether too subtle for my intelligence. I still could not think of anything more that I could usefully do!

That evening, Baker Street had a caller. Being Thursday, and around seven o'clock, I would normally have guessed it to be Lestrade, who often seemed to favour that time and day. In view of what I'd read that morning, I thought it unlikely – but I was wrong. It was Lestrade, and Lestrade looking, I thought, unexpectedly pleased with himself!

He'd obviously come to see Holmes but, despite being told that Holmes might still be some time in returning, he appeared to be in no hurry to leave. Having smoked half a cigar and complained about the chaos which still existed at the Yard as a result of the bombing, he intimated that after the kindness which had been shown to him on his last visit, he'd thought that Holmes might be interested in some surprising new developments in the affair which had been the cause of his earlier embarrassment.

"I've read the article in *Judy*," I said, unthinkingly and, I instantly realised, rather tactlessly. Yet Lestrade appeared unconcerned!

"That successful robbery," he said, "was only the first. There've been three more since – in different places, but each in almost identical circumstances, each, it seems, made possible by 'silent canaries'!"

It was not the information which surprised me half so much as Lestrade's attitude. Indeed, he was actually smiling!

"You'll forgive my saying it, Dr Watson, but you do not possess Mr Holmes' ability to disguise your reactions completely. You are wondering, after reading that very unpleasant personal and, as you know, unfair attack upon me, why I have anything to be pleased about. And since I doubt whether even your friend Mr Holmes could deduce the answer to that, I will tell you.

"I'm sure that I do not have to explain that a series of unsuccessful robberies, followed by a series of successful ones, all of them associated with canaries, is a highly suspicious circumstance. It becomes doubly so when coupled with the knowledge that this man, Archibold Wilson, has a long criminal record – including a strong suspicion of a double child murder! Admittedly to my surprise, I was today summoned by my superiors, not to receive an expected reprimand, but to be assigned to take complete charge of this investigation."

It was also "to *my* surprise", but I did now understand the reason for Lestrade's visit – the hope that Holmes might proffer some ideas! I thought it only fair at least to tell him that though Holmes had shown some interest he was totally committed to this business of "The Dynamiters". He had, however, asked me to make a few enquiries on his behalf.

At that point, Lestrade remarked only that as Holmes had not returned, there was perhaps little point in his staying longer. Whilst it is very possible that I was merely being oversensitive, I had the sudden feeling that Lestrade did not regard anything I might have contributed to the investigation as even worth the hearing. I could certainly disillusion him upon that! I suggested that he might like to enjoy another cigar while I gave him a summary of what he must soon realise to be my very considerable knowledge of canaries!

I noticed that he was at least impressed enough to make copious notes and, when at last he did leave, it was with what appeared to be a genuine sense of gratitude for my assistance.

Chapter Five

A Remarkable Demonstration

Once more I had gone to my bed before Holmes returned, with the consequence that I had no opportunity to discuss with him either the article which he had left me, or Lestrade's visit. In direct consequence of that, I spent a wakeful night, much of it occupied in contemplation of my wisdom, or lack of it, in telling Lestrade as much as I had. By morning, I had convinced myself that my motive had been no other than one of quite childish self-indulgence. And I had determined to confess my sins to Holmes over breakfast.

His reaction was almost disappointing, in that he clearly did not regard it as anything over which I need have lost any sleep. He was, on the contrary, pleased!

"I confess, Watson," he said, "that I had found myself in some difficulty. The successful burglary which was described in the article, I had assumed to be the first of several. That, Lestrade has confirmed. And you are also correct in your assumption that these burglaries are exactly the kind of development that I had been anticipating. But then came my difficulty.

"I had promised that the Wilson Case was yours and that I would not interfere further. But, Watson, you may also recall that on that occasion when I first broached the matter with you, I also promised that I would not ask the impossible of you. I feared that I was doing just that! I really should have realised that if my assumptions were correct, you would need to have access to the scenes of the crimes which were surely about to take place. That might have been difficult for me, but for you, Watson, as I have said, 'impossible'. But, thanks to your conversation yesterday with Lestrade, I no longer see a problem."

I could not see why that should be so.

"Only because you do not yet know Lestrade as I do. The man may have only limited abilities, but he is a conscientious policeman. I'm sure that he spares no effort in attempting to solve the cases which he is given. And he has more than usual reason to succeed in solving this one. Not only has he been made to look a fool, but he has now been given the quite unexpected opportunity both to obtain personal redress, and to serve the ends of justice. It was inevitable that he should come here seeking my ideas."

"Because he probably has none of his own!"

"On the contrary, Watson, I'm sure that Lestrade came here thinking that he could already see the direction which his investigation should follow. He was merely seeking my confirmation."

"But you weren't here."

"True. But you were, and you provided that confirmation – with your comprehensive account of the methods by which canaries are trained."

I still did not understand.

"It's difficult to explain, and I wouldn't wish to cloud your own thinking, Watson. I should prefer it to be fresh! Merely be assured that Lestrade, having painstakingly checked upon a few more details, will feel supremely confident of his theories – and without the help of Sherlock Holmes! If I judge my man aright, he will be unable to resist sharing his moment of triumph. And, in all the circumstances, who more obvious a choice of audience than your good self? That will, I hope, provide you with the opportunity to supply me with the one last answer that I need to put an end to the activities of Mr Archibold Wilson – I trust for some time!"

....

It was just three days later that I received a note from Lestrade, asking if I would care to join him at nine o'clock that evening at an address in Charles Street, off St James's Square. He apologised for the lateness of the hour – explaining that darkness was required for the purpose of the demonstration which he had arranged, but assured me that he was certain I would find it rewarding. I showed the note to Holmes, who happened to be at home at the time of its arrival.

"You must, of course, accept, Watson," was Holmes' first comment, He added, "Notably, the invitation is not extended to myself and I would, in any event, most probably be unavailable at that time. You will be pleased to know, Watson, that I am very close to solving the last of my problems in relation to the use of finger prints. And, in truth, I am tired and anxious only to see the business out of the way with as much despatch as possible."

I said that I understood. I also understood that Holmes did attach some importance to the matter of Wilson. I knew that only good fortune had prevented my ruining things already with a display of false pride – and I was not about to repeat that mistake. "You know," I said, "that you will have to tell me exactly what you want me to do."

"I can't tell you 'exactly'," Holmes answered. "I imagine that Lestrade is hoping to demonstrate how it is possible to 'turn off' a canary burglar alarm. Whether or not he succeeds should be obvious. And that may be all that I need to know. What else can I advise, except to suggest that you take a lesson from the young constable who visited us at the very beginning of this affair. Try to remember *everything* that you see or hear. Let me decide what is important!"

....

Charles Street is typical of much of Westminster –

Georgian terraces comprising a mixture of private residences and public buildings, either fronting directly onto the pavements, or separated from them by basement entrances. It had been a wet day and was getting quite dark on my arrival. Lestrade met me in the hall – looking troubled.

"I hope," he said, "that you are not going to be disappointed, Dr Watson. Clearly, I should have given this Wilson man credit for being rather more clever than I'd supposed, though I assure you it is only a matter of time."

"Time for what?" I asked.

"Discovering precisely how the cage works!"

I have no doubt that I continued to look blank.

"Ah!" Lestrade responded. "I had assumed that though Mr Holmes has had little time for this case, he might well have suspected that the key to the mystery lay in the so-called audiophonic cage. But no matter. If you will come upstairs with me to the drawing room, Dr Watson, I shall explain."

On the way to the drawing room Lestrade did also explain some other things, one of which had already begun to puzzle me – the apparent absence of any owners of the house. It was, he told me, the residence of Sir Basil and Lady Shallcross. "Sir Basil is in the Diplomatic Service. He *was* on home leave, but he's been suddenly re-called to Egypt. I'm told that this prophet of Allah is still busy stirring up rebellion among the Sudanese. I'd have thought when they sent 'Chinese' Gordon out there, that would have been an end to it, but it seems it isn't. So, Doctor, the house is empty, apart from two staff, my constable and myself." We had entered the drawing room. Standing on a table was what I recognised as a Wilson Audiophonic Canary Cage.

"This house was burgled last week – another case of a 'silent canary'. That's not the cage. It's from the scene of another burglary. We've been examining it at the Yard. And I can tell you this, Doctor. It doesn't do anything – at least nothing that it's claimed to do in the advertisements. The experts tell us that it might just work if the canary sat exactly where it's shown in the picture, and didn't move, but you'd still be hard pushed to notice any difference!"

"Which," I said, "is why you assume that the cage must, therefore, be intended to do something else."

"One of the reasons, Dr Watson. You see, the professional policeman does have certain advantages even over the most gifted amateur. Our conclusions don't rely on some sudden inspiration. First we collect all of the facts – some of those facts not even available to the amateur. And then we draw our conclusions. Slow it may be, but it means that when we do draw our conclusions, then we're not relying upon guesswork."

Lestrade was clearly enjoying himself, having a sly dig, not at myself, but at Holmes, who was not there to answer him. As I was there to learn what I could, I could not afford to offend Lestrade. I had to let him go on, unchallenged.

"There was, of course, the possibility that all Wilson was seeking to do was to make a large profit out of a device which simply didn't work."

I thought to tell Lestrade that even I had seen that possibility, but didn't.

"We know that isn't the explanation. I've taken some advice on just what it would cost to make one of these cages. The price at which Wilson is selling them can hardly cover that cost."

I did remember telling Holmes how cheap I thought they were. I was now glad that I had said nothing to Lestrade!

"And that isn't all, Doctor. You know that there've recently been a large number of attempted burglaries in the Westminster area, twenty-three to be exact. Five were successful, eighteen unsuccessful. Every house but one had one of these Wilson Canaries. Every successful burglary has been in a house which had not only a canary, but also one of these cages!"

The conclusions did seem to be inescapable. Wilson had arranged the "unsuccessful" burglaries to prove the worth of the canaries, and to encourage people to pay the very reasonable extra charge for purchasing the audiophonic cage. Somehow, the cage made it possible for the burglar to enter without the canary raising the alarm. One other thing had just struck me. It seemed to be a great deal of trouble to go to, just to commit a very few burglaries. "Surely," I said to Lestrade, "no one will now buy Wilson's cages or his canaries, at least, not as burglar alarms!"

"Oh! But they will, Doctor! You obviously haven't seen the latest advertisement in today's newspapers."

I certainly hadn't noticed one.

"I haven't a copy to show you, but I can remember the gist. It goes something like: 'No one can give you an absolute guarantee to protect your home from attempted burglary. But almost four out of five owners of a Wilson Trained Canary can expect that any such attempt will be unsuccessful.'"

"It's clever!" I said.

"Too clever!" Lestrade replied. "People will go on buying Wilson Canaries, houses will go on being robbed, and I can't stop it! I can't even put a constable into a house in the hopes of catching the thieves red-handed. I don't know where the cages are going, or when. And if I did, I still wouldn't know which houses were going to be robbed! I'll tell you, Dr Watson, Wilson is getting a valuable haul from every house he robs. He'll not need to do many more before he's a rich man. And I can't even put the heavy hand on him, not without evidence. It's the cage! I know it's the cage!"

Lestrade was becoming quite agitated. I reminded him that I was here to see a demonstration, and that it was now quite dark. With a visible effort, Lestrade recovered his composure.

"I'm sorry, Doctor. The demonstration will be in the next room, the one which was entered through the window and robbed, last week. The bird and its cage are still there."

"Entered through the window," I repeated, feeling that might be important and something upon which Holmes might well question me.

"No doubt," Lestrade replied. "You can still see the marks where the window catch was forced, and there are marks on the window ledge. There was no need to look any further. And they let themselves out again through the back door. But now, I'll surprise you, Doctor. Maybe you wonder why I asked *you* here. I'll tell you. It's because I like to give credit where it's due. And it was you, Dr Watson who put me on the right track in this business."

"I?" I queried in some disbelief.

"You, Doctor, by telling me how canaries are trained to sing when required – by exposing them to light! So you can see what happened in those houses where everyone supposes that it was the canary that scared off the burglars. One of Wilson's men climbs up to the window, forces it open, then shines a lantern at the canary. The canary starts to sing. The 'burglar' leaves – and also leaves the householder convinced that he has been saved by the canary!

"And then comes the clever bit! If the canary is in one of these 'Audiophonic Cages', then there's some way to prevent it from singing – even if you shine a light on it. I don't yet know how, perhaps a galvanic shock. But I can still demonstrate the principle, if you'll come with me, Dr Watson."

We left the drawing room and walked to the next room, stopping outside the closed door. Lestrade had brought a lighted oil lamp with us.

"Let me first explain something," Lestrade said. "These audiophonic cages are always delivered in a wooden crate. The crate is taken away when they're finished, so I can't show you one. But that's not important."

I agreed. I'd seen one of the crates in Wilson's shop – nothing more than a simple white-wood packing case. Lestrade continued.

"The purpose of bringing the cage in a crate is so that it can be assembled in the room of the house where it is to be used. Whoever brings and assembles it has plenty of time, first to decide whether the place is worth robbing, and second to memorise the position of the cage and the other furniture in the room. The burglar has to get from the window to the cage – in the dark. I don't yet know how the cage works, but I propose to use a makeshift device to produce the same effect. My constable will now make certain that there's no light showing from downstairs. If you, Doctor, will take this lamp and be ready to extinguish it when I tell you. You have matches?"

I had.

"I have memorised the furniture inside this room, which is, of course, already in darkness.

Please extinguish your lamp, and I will tell you when you may relight it."

In what now seemed to be total blackness, I heard Lestrade open the door of the room and close it again – I assumed behind him. A short silence was followed by muffled sounds, and what might have been a few quiet oaths! Perhaps Lestrade had not memorised the positions of the furniture as accurately as he'd imagined! After what seemed like a considerable time, I heard the door open once more and Lestrade's voice telling me to relight the lamp and come into the room.

My first reaction upon entering the room was to realise that though the lamp was lit, there was certainly no sound of a canary singing. My second reaction was to wonder why I could see neither a canary nor a cage. Lestrade was smiling, as pleasantly as Lestrade ever could.

"Not magic, Dr Watson. Merely a crude, but very simple device."

He stepped across the room to some tall object, draped in a heavy cloth. I was beginning to guess what he'd done when, with something of a flourish, he seized the cloth and pulled it away – to reveal a floor-standing ormolu oil lamp, complete with large silk shade! Lestrade was no longer smiling. He turned slowly about, clearly attempting to find his bearings, then stepped towards a generously upholstered chair, just a little to his right. I was near enough to see something of what had happened. The metal stand which had supported the birdcage was lying by the chair on the well-carpeted floor. The cage itself, apparently now upside down, was on the seat of the chair. Closer inspection revealed the unfortunate canary to be alive, but crouched in a position suggesting a state of some terror, whilst a mixture of seed and water spread slowly across the fine brocade of the chair's upholstery.

In the darkness, Lestrade had clearly missed his target, covering only the lamp with the cloth and knocking over the cage and stand, but in a manner which had created too little noise for him to have realised exactly what he had done. I was having very considerable difficulty in restraining my laughter. If not exactly in the manner intended, Lestrade had, indeed, silenced the canary! The situation was probably saved by the sudden appearance of an elderly woman whose dress suggested her to be one of the servants of whom Lestrade had spoken. She had probably come only to ask how long we might be expected to remain in the house but, whatever her original purpose, her attention was now focussed perhaps less on the plight of the canary than on the damage already caused to the chair's upholstery.

Lestrade was apologetic, quickly excusing himself from the room on the pretext of wishing to speak to his constable. I helped the woman to remove the cage, whereupon she used the cloth Lestrade had wrapped around the lamp to mop up some of the seed and water.

Feeling a need to break the tense silence, I said, "I trust the shock to the bird won't have any lasting effects on its singing ability."

"I'd not say as it's got much of that, anyway," the woman answered. "It's better than the first one. That didn't never utter a note, not in my hearing. When I were a girl, my mother was buying me a linnet in the Greenwich market, for four pence, and it were a better singer than either of them canaries."

"You said, 'either of them – those – canaries'?"

Lestrade and his youthful constable had returned to the room.

"Yes, sir. I was telling this gentleman. After we was having the robbery, the man who sells us the bird is coming back. Says that either the bird or the cage, or both, must be faulty. Offered to take them back and return the money. But the mistress wants a canary, for the singing. So we gets a new cage and a new canary. But I'm saying –"

She didn't finish. Lestrade had interrupted.

"It's not the original cage. And for all I know the cage that's been all this time at the Yard's not the original cage. Why did nobody find that out!"

Lestrade sounded as if he were about to get rid of some of his anger and frustration – on his constable. I thought it time to leave. I did say my 'goodnights' and express my thanks, but Lestrade may not have heard me. He was loudly lecturing his constable upon the subject of being surrounded by fools!

Chapter Six

In which Holmes' Hand is Forced

When I reached Baker Street, it was to find that Holmes had also returned. He insisted that I sit myself down and, then and there, relate every detail of what had happened while all of it was still fresh in my memory. When I'd finished, he asked only one thing – that I describe the canary! I did, to the best of my ability. I knew there were different varieties of canary but, since to me, they were still just yellow birds, I couldn't see the reason for his interest.

"I'm obliged to you, Watson," he said. "I now have the answer to the last of my questions. It therefore remains only for me to find a suitable opportunity to conclude the case."

"You are saying, Holmes, that you know how the cage works."

"Not in the way you mean it, Watson. Very simply, the cage doesn't work. It doesn't do anything!"

If I looked confused, it was because I felt it!

"You find that difficult to believe – for two reasons. You were impressed with Lestrade's logic. And if Lestrade's logic is wrong, then one would appear to be left with a situation in which there *is* no other possible explanation."

I agreed, or I *thought* I agreed!

"I confess," Holmes said, "that I am myself impressed with Lestrade's logic. I had not thought the man capable of it. It is unfortunate that it is so faultless in every respect but one – the original assumption upon which it is based. He was rightly suspicious of the fact that Wilson would appear to be selling his cages at little or no profit. But he mistook the reason."

"And you are going to tell me the reason."

"Not tonight, Watson, because it would spoil the pleasure for you. I intend to show you the reason – I trust, very shortly. My work for Scotland Yard is very nearly completed. Indeed, by tomorrow evening, I hope to give you a first viewing of my endeavours, and you could assist me in that."

"How?" I asked.

"Tomorrow," Holmes answered, "I shall be setting up at the Yard a small exhibition of my work on finger prints. Since I expect it to be met with some scepticism, and therefore wishing my presentation to be simple and clear, not to say, attractive, I have commissioned some large diagrams which are being prepared for me by a small business in Northumberland Place. I had hoped the work would be completed by this evening. It was not, but is promised for eleven in the morning."

"You wish me to collect it."

"I do, Watson, and if you would be so kind, to bring it to Scotland Yard."

....

I collected the work for Holmes and duly delivered it to Scotland Yard. Because he could not know where he would be in the Yard's scattered buildings when I arrived, he had arranged for one of the desk sergeants to receive and take care of it for him. My only difficulty proved to be the transporting of the material from the cab into the building. It was not heavy, but some of it was large, restricting my vision so that I collided with a young constable while negotiating some double doors. As I made my apologies, I recognised the constable as the young man whom I had last seen on the previous evening receiving the sharp edge of Lestrade's tongue! I thought that the constable might feel better if I showed that I had ignored that incident. So, not expecting an answer of any real interest, I asked merely whether, in having had to leave at the time I did, I had missed anything of any importance.

The answer to my precise question was just as I expected, but not the information which followed it! The constable might have been speaking out of turn, though I'm sure that his intention was, in fact, only to defend what he saw as his superior's slightly hysterical behaviour.

"Detective Sergeant Lestrade was very upset," he said. "The Sergeant's a hard-working officer and a good detective. Being a policeman's difficult enough without feeling it's your own colleagues who've let you down."

I said that I fully understood – and thought that this young man would go far in the police force!

"But," he added, "you might say that Sergeant Lestrade has had a stroke of good luck. You know, sir, what it was that was most upsetting him last night."

I thought I did. He was convinced that the solution to the robberies lay in the construction of the cages. But he had discovered that the cage he'd been examining might not have been the same cage that was there at the time of the robbery.

"Just so, sir," was the constable's reply. "Well, this morning, he's passing a house in St James's Square, and he sees one of these cages being delivered, on a cart – the crate being painted with the words, 'Wilson's Bird Emporium'. He knows the house its going to and he knows that if there's any house in St James's Square that's worth robbing, it's that one! I'd not be knowing whether what he did is allowed under the law, but I think I'd have taken the same chance. He confiscates the crate and has it brought here to the Yard!"

"And he's discovered its secret?"

"I don't know that, sir. I haven't seen Sergeant Lestrade since just after the cage arrived here."

....

Holmes was early in returning to Baker Street that evening, early enough to join me in our evening meal. He seemed to have brought a great deal of paper home with him – sufficient to require the cab driver to assist him in bringing all of it upstairs to our rooms. He looked a deal more relaxed than I had seen him in a long time and insisted that we ate together before even looking at what he'd brought to show me. He did thank me for delivering the material to the Yard that morning and it was inevitable that I should tell him about Lestrade having confiscated a cage as it was being delivered to a house. Holmes' only comment was that it was "a pity" – it was doubtful whether Lestrade had any legal right to have done so, and he would find the action difficult to defend. Holmes clearly remained convinced that the cage was nothing more than it appeared. Lestrade would uncover no secrets in it, because there were none!

When we had finished our meal and Mrs Hudson had cleared the table, Holmes began to spread out some of the papers which he had brought home with him – so far as I could see, a mixture of diagrams and photographs. The table and Holmes' desk were not large enough to accommodate them. Chair seats were filled and the rest spread out on the floor.

"You know what I have been trying to do," Holmes began, "to devise methods of making visible and photographing the finger prints of anyone who has handled an object, to find a simple, reliable way of classifying those prints, and to apply that knowledge to the several complete and innumerable parts of bombs which the police have now accumulated.

"While certain aspects of my work could still be improved upon, I consider myself largely successful in all those aims. I have no names – only people whom I identify as 'person A', 'person B', and so on. What I can tell you about them is the part which each one played in the making or delivering of the bombs, and I can discern certain connections between them."

That explanation brought me to a point which I had reached once before. I thought that I could appreciate what Holmes was saying, but I could not see its practical value.

"Very simply this, Watson. There is no doubt that some of these bombers will be caught and brought to trial. It is equally certain that those arrested will have known associates – but against whom there is no evidence. What I have done is to provide that evidence. If a man is caught planting a bomb and the finger prints of one of his known associates can be shown on some part of that bomb then –"

Unaccountably, Holmes stopped in mid-sentence.

"Watson," he said. "When we were eating, you told me that Lestrade had confiscated a cage

which was about to be delivered to a house in
St James's Square."

"I did."

"When you told me that, you said a 'cage'. Was
it, in fact, only a cage, or a cage which had yet to
be unpacked and assembled from its crate?"

It was, of course, the latter. I probably had said
'cage', though I could not see that it was of great
importance.

"If Lestrade was wrong in guessing that the
intention was to rob that house, then it may not
be of importance," Holmes answered. "But if
Lestrade was correct in his assumption, then I fear
that something is very wrong. Either I should
have heard something at the Yard, or Lestrade
should have arrived here in person – certainly by
now. Get your coat Watson. The evening has
turned quite chill."

I asked what we were to do with all the papers
which were strewn about the room,

"Leave them," was the reply. "If I am right,
Watson, we may have no time to lose!"

....

Fifteen minutes later we were back at Scotland
Yard, with Holmes making enquiries as to the
whereabouts of Lestrade. It was established that
Lestrade was somewhere in the Paddington area.
There had been a bomb alert earlier in the even-
ing. Lestrade was one of several officers from the
Yard who had been dispatched to the area. He
had not returned. Holmes turned his enquiries to

what had befallen the crate which Lestrade had had brought to the Yard that morning. Perhaps because Lestrade's unfortunate connections with canaries and cages was something of a standing joke in Scotland Yard, the whereabouts of the cage was quickly established – but not the crate in which it had arrived. I still did not understand Holmes' interest in the crate, but he was becoming increasingly frustrated that no one had any knowledge of its present whereabouts.

Half an hour later something *was* established about its possible fate. Someone did recollect having seen what he described as a "large, empty, mahogany box" standing in a corridor – together with an irate senior officer who, having just barked his shins on it, was ordering that it be removed, to "anywhere", as long as it was out of the way! More than that, no one knew. Though I suggested to Holmes that it didn't sound like the crate we were looking for, he insisted upon an immediate search of the building. The search revealed nothing. But, with there being several other buildings which, together, made up Scotland Yard, it might have been put anywhere in any one of them. It could take many hours to find it.

Minutes later, Holmes had bundled me out of the Yard and into another cab, in which we proceeded at breakneck speed to Bishopsgate Street Without, Sherlock Holmes continually urging our driver to "go faster".

At near ten o'clock at night, Wilson's Emporium of Singing Birds was inevitably closed. It did not prevent Holmes from hammering on the door with his stick, with a force that threatened to break the glass in it. It did bring a quick response – a window on the first floor over the shop was thrown up and a head and shoulders stuck out to discover the cause of the uproar. Even in the fading light, I recognised the face that stared down at us as that of Archibold Wilson.

Respecting the possible sensitivity of some of my readers, I shan't recount exactly the exchange of words which then took place. Suffice it to say that it began with Wilson threatening to call the police and ended with his opening the shop door when Holmes offered to save him the trouble by calling the police himself!

"I wants no trouble. I tries to run an honest business, like you might say on the side of the law – being as I been preventin' crime. It's that Sergeant Lestrade, isn't it! Can't solve none of these robberies that's been happenin' – and so blames them on me! Says as it's my canary cages. He don't know what mark you, just he's sure as it's the cages. Stops me this morning just when I'm a deliverin' one. Takes it away, 'steals' it I'd say, and right in front of the house of one of the best customers I'm ever havin'!

"I heard of you, Mr Holmes. And from what I hears, I wouldn't have thought you'd be one for falling for anything that Lestrade's been tellin' you. I got a shop full o' cages. You don't 'ave to steal one, Mr Holmes. Help yourself. You won't find nothing!"

Holmes had gained admittance to the shop with a barrage of words. But after that it was a nervous and discernably agitated Wilson who had done all of the talking. It seemed that perhaps he had now finished, but that the cause was myself! The shop was lit by a single oil lamp which Wilson had with him when he had opened the door. I must have stepped closer to it, giving him, for the first time, clear sight of my face.

"I never seen you, Mr Holmes, before," he said, "but I know this gentleman, don't I?"

Holmes answered for me.

"The possibility of your recognising my colleague, Dr Watson, is as unlikely as it is unimportant. I am not here to waste time, and I do not wish to examine your cages because I am certain that I will find in them nothing of interest."

Wilson managed a half smile, perhaps of relief tinged with curiosity.

"My interest lies in the wooden crates in which they are packed – or should I say, in one particular wooden crate, the one taken this morning by Sergeant Lestrade to Scotland Yard. I want to know exactly where it is at this moment."

The smile remained but had taken on a fixed, unnatural appearance.

"You're joking with me, Mr Holmes. How should I know more than that it's still at Scotland

Yard? But if it's wooden boxes you wants to see, I got plenty of them as well as –"

The next word merged into a startled gasp. Holmes stood a foot taller than Wilson. He had grasped the man by the front of his clothes and, with one hand, lifted him bodily from the floor so that they were staring into each other's faces.

"Where?" Holmes repeated.

"You're mad! I've told you –"

Holmes had raised the stick which he carried in his other hand.

"Where?"

"Honest – I don't know!"

Holmes had lowered the man to the ground and was pressing him back against the shop counter. Suddenly, the stick came down, missing Wilson, but crashing onto the counter!

"Where?"

The stick was raised again.

"The building next to the Rising Sun. There's a narrow entry on the other side. There's a door on the right, a few yards in. It's a cellar. I don't know no more than that, I swear I don't!"

Holmes released his grasp. Wilson slid to the floor. I moved towards the man to see whether he was all right, but Holmes had taken my arm and dragged me from the shop.

"I thought you were going to kill him, Holmes!"

"It was necessary that Wilson believed that I might. We must find a cab, Watson. Perhaps our chances will be better if we go to Liverpool Street

Station. Hurry, Watson, and listen carefully to what I say. We need a doctor."

"I *am* a doctor!"

"Don't be difficult, Watson, and don't interrupt! We need a doctor who can treat a patient at some place other than Baker Street. And it must be someone in whom you have absolute trust."

I could think only of Anstruther.

"We were at Barts together. He has a small practice in Paddington. I don't know him that well – but I think that I could trust him. I would know better if I knew what it is you require of him!"

"No time. Here's paper and pencil. Write the address for me. I will take the first cab that we find. You will take the second and go to Anstruther. We must just hope that he is at home."

"But what do I tell him, Holmes? I must tell him something!"

"Tell him that you are both to await my arrival. Tell him to pray that we may still be in time to save a life!"

Chapter Seven

A Conflict of Reason

It is more likely to have been Holmes' reputation than my slight friendship, which eventually persuaded Anstruther to agree to participate in something about which I could tell him very little more than the cryptic message with which Holmes had left me.

Holmes himself arrived at Anstruther's house at a little before midnight. He forewent the formality of introductions in his haste to have us help him unload a wooden crate from his cab. The crate was surprisingly heavy. I assumed this was because it was made of mahogany. Other than in size and shape, it bore no resemblance to the simple, quite crudely made, white-wood packing case which I had seen in Wilson's shop. Mahogany did seem to be an unusually expensive and heavy wood to use for the purpose.

Holmes asked that it be carried directly to

Anstruther's surgery! There he removed his jacket, got down on his knees and, with the aid of his magnifying glass, began to examine the crate with what was clearly deep concentration!

"Our first problem is to open it," he said. "It will, doubtless, be some quite simple mechanism – but cunningly disguised."

Anstruther gave me a curious glance. I had no doubt that he could see what I could see myself – four screws, already partly loosened. Were they to be removed, it was obvious that one side of the crate could then be lifted off! Holmes' attention was devoted to the *opposite* side of the crate and I could only assume that he had, for once, missed the obvious. I should have known better!

"If you must satisfy your curiosity, Watson," he said, not shifting his attention, "do remove the front of the crate, but before you do it, perhaps you or Dr Anstruther would find me something with a narrow blade. A pocket knife would do."

Anstruther handed him a pocket knife while I removed the four loose screws from the front of the crate and lifted it off.

"It's empty," I said.

Holmes ignored me. Suddenly he stood up, holding what appeared to be the back wall of the crate in his hands. I should now have been able to see right through it. I could not. From my side, the back wall appeared to be still in place! Before I could say anything, Holmes had spoken to Anstruther, who was standing nearer to him.

"Tell me first," he said, quietly, "whether or not the child is still alive."

....

If I had not seen it, I would not have believed it possible that a human body, albeit that of a child, could be confined within so small a space. The head and body were between the back wall of the crate, which Holmes had removed, and a false wall – the one which I could still see from the front, which gave the crate the appearance of being empty. The upper part of the child's legs were in the sitting position, but were bent completely back at the knees so that the calfs, heels and soles of the feet touched the thighs and buttocks. The legs were also splayed out so that they could occupy two tiny compartments which lay hidden in either side of what, from the front, looked like straw packing with a circular well at its centre to hold the base of the bird cage. The illusion of the crate being empty was further heightened by various wooden fixtures screwed to the false back wall. These were used to hold the parts of the cage.

"He *is* alive," Anstruther pronounced, "but barely. There can't have been much air getting in, and I don't like the colour of the legs. How long has he been in there?"

"Perhaps sixteen hours," Holmes answered. "The child's life is now in your hands, gentlemen and if there is nothing more I can do to assist at this time, it may be better that I leave you."

....

It was more than an hour later before I rejoined Holmes in Anstruther's living room, where he had waited.

"The child has been conscious," I told him, "though only briefly. That is perhaps a blessing. The pain of restoring the circulation in his legs will be very great. Thank God, he will not lose them."

Holmes gave a questioning look.

"There was some doubt," I explained. "If the circulation of blood had totally ceased, then the limbs could have become gangrenous. Amputation would have been the only possible course, though I doubt whether he could have withstood the shock of such an operation."

"How much longer could he have been in there and survived?"

"Difficult," I answered. "At best, an hour."

"But he will recover?"

"He has a very good chance – given time and careful nursing. His general physical condition is pitifully poor. The child has been half starved – I assume to ensure that he could be squeezed into the monstrous contraption that so very nearly became his tomb!"

Holmes was silent for a moment.

"The nursing of the child, perhaps his eventual placement with some respectable family, could it be arranged? The money would, of course, be provided, but it would have to be done with absolute discretion."

I said that I was sure it would be possible.

"Then do it for me, Watson. I shall return to Baker Street and wait for you there."

....

It was dawn when I left Anstruther's house and myself returned to 221B. Holmes was still up, but insisted that I take a few hours' sleep. It was advice I was glad to take and it was two that same afternoon before I woke, dressed and came down to our living room. Holmes was still seated in exactly the position I had left him that morning. I asked if he had slept, but he ignored my question.

"I wasn't certain, Watson," he said, "not till we had visited Wilson last night – though why else would he have used a mahogany box instead of one of the cheap, whitewood crates he showed to you? The fact that he was still at the shop, meant one of two things. The crate was, indeed, empty – or it was not, but he still felt safe from discovery. I could only be sure that it was the latter when he told me exactly where it was."

"But how *did* he know where it was?" I asked.

"His children, Watson. You may be sure that he dispatched some of them to Scotland Yard to wait and watch. He knew that the presence of the child in the box was unlikely to be discovered. The means of opening the hidden compartment was well concealed. The material of which the crate was made was sufficient to account for its weight. Once it had been consigned to a cellar, he was safe, at least for the moment."

"But the child," I said. "He must have been concerned about the child!"

Quite unexpectedly, Holmes laughed!

"Oh! Watson! You still don't know. You still can't believe the depth of evil in this man. He knew the child would die – and cared nothing. Today, he would have appeared at Scotland Yard, full of false indignation, to reclaim his property. And it would surely have been returned to him, corpse and all!

"So I've saved one child. A note arrived from Anstruther while you slept. Arrangements have already been made for the child to be cared for. You, Watson, no doubt see it as an act of humanity. Yet I know it to be against all reason!"

I didn't understand. I told Holmes that he had done a fine thing.

"You say so. That child's testimony and the crate in which he very nearly died, were my only solid evidence against Wilson, my only means of putting him behind bars for a very long time. Yet if I ever reveal my knowledge of the child's existence, he will surely have to go to court. The fact that he would appear as Queen's evidence, would not prevent his being consigned to some institution that would not offer him the care which you, Watson, tell me is needed to save his life.

"Without the child, there is no evidence. In any event, you may be certain that Wilson is gone from his emporium, is already many miles from here. And he remains free, Watson – free to pursue his evil ways, free to bring like suffering, even death, to many more children who may in the future be unfortunate enough to cross his path."

I told Holmes that I understood his feelings, but that he had no choice. I found it remarkable enough that he had saved one child – in a case which he had solved before ever having had any personal involvement in it!

"Don't humour me, old friend. The solution of the case was so childishly simple that I can take little credit even for that."

It may have been "childishly simple" for Holmes. It was not for me – and since I had, I believed, assisted in the solution, I hoped that I might at least be given some explanation. Holmes became suddenly apologetic.

"You are right, Watson. Of course, you are enti-tled to that explanation, though you will see that it was, indeed, simple. That something curious was afoot became instantly apparent upon your first showing me the advertisement for the cage."

I now remembered that Holmes had indeed said so at the time. I still did not see why.

"The timing, Watson. Lestrade told us that the 'unsuccessful burglaries' which had, allegedly, inspired the first canary advertisement, had hap-pened 'in the last two months'. The advertise-ment for the 'Audiophonic Cage' appeared only some two weeks after the first advertisement. Such a cage, obviously of new and unique design, could not possibly have been conceived and manufactured in such a short space of time. It had to have been produced *before* the incidents which were supposed to have inspired it had occurred!"

From my single visit to Wilson's Emporium, Holmes had deduced much of what it had taken Lestrade a deal longer to discover. The fact that no cage was already assembled for demonstration in the shop, confirmed what Holmes suspected – that the cage did not do what the advertisement claimed of it. Its cheapness suggested that there was a reason for Wilson wishing to sell these cages at little or no profit. The cages were uncrated and assembled "on site", an obvious device for giving would-be thieves the opportunity of examining the layout and contents of the premises. But, even at that time, Holmes was wondering about the crates. My chance remark about the crate being carried into the shop by two boys, "one hardly bigger than the crate", had reminded him of an old fairground illusion in which a girl is produced from an apparently empty box!

The subsequent outbreak of successful burglaries, due it seemed to silent canaries, had put a doubt in Holmes' mind – though he was reluctant to believe that the canaries' silence was attributable to the cage.

"Your visit to Charles Street resolved that matter," he told me.

I would not have thought that conclusive. "There was the possibility," I said, "that Lestrade had not examined an original cage."

"Oh! It wasn't the cage, Watson. It was the canary. Your description, and the servant's remarks convinced me of the true solution."

"You've lost me, Holmes!"

"You said the canary was yellow."

"It was. Well they are, aren't they?"

"Usually, though the famous roller canaries bred in the Harz Mountains, are almost invariably green, the original colour of their wild ancestors. They are also highly prized and highly priced. You see, Watson, even without training, any canary will sing, though it will not perform to order. But it was really the servant's observations which gave me the vital clue. As I'd always suspected, the whole business of the audiophonic cage and the canary burglar alarm was no more than a clever diversion to distract attention from the simple truth. Much easier than stopping a canary from singing, is merely to provide one which will never sing at all!"

"But you said they all sang."

"All males. Hen canaries rarely do, and never when they are broody."

What Holmes had said could not account for the attempted burglaries where the canary had roused the household.

"Those, Watson, *were* male canaries – though I doubt if any of them roused anyone. The 'burglars', having forced a window, themselves provided the alarm – with a 'bird organ', a device of which I'm sure you've read.

"When an actual burglary was intended, the procedure was quite different. It would first have been established that the house was worth robbing – such information being most easily obtained from the servants. In these cases, the cage would be delivered in the specially constructed mahogany crate – with the boy installed inside it. If, after entering the house, it still looked to be as suitable for burglary as the information had suggested, then an opportunity would be created to release the boy from the crate and hide him somewhere in the house itself. The canary which was left was a broody hen, the household being told, as you were, Watson, that because of the strangeness of its surroundings, the bird might not sing immediately.

"That night, Wilson or his confederates would be let into the house by the boy, and would leave the same way. The marks on the window catch and ledge, suggesting forced entry, were made from inside the room. Lestrade was so convinced that he failed to check the ground outside, where he'd have found a significant absence of evidence! If the householder complained about the bird not singing, their money was refunded, or the hen was replaced by a male canary, which might, like Shallcross's replacement, still prove to be an indifferent singer!"

Holmes seemed to have explained everything – except the means by which he had obtained the crate from the cellar in Scotland Yard and brought it by cab to Anstruther's house.

"A little bluff, Watson. When one is known to have been commissioned to assist the police by that most gracious and emminent of persons, it would seem that Her Majesty's police officers are anxious, or feel obliged, to offer you every assistance. You saw it last night when we visited the Yard together. I merely said that I had a crate in the cellar containing parts of bombs which I wished to examine at Baker Street. I know that I shall have to be equally inventive if Lestrade ever makes enquiries as to the fate of the crate which he had brought to the Yard."

I was sorely tempted to ask Holmes whether the "assistance" of which he had just spoken, might have extended to his persuading someone to take a more than generous attitude towards Lestrade. I had never quite seen why, far from being reprimanded, Lestrade had actually been assigned to a case where his only contribution till then, had been to bring the police into further disrepute! But I did not ask. I did not want to appear to be accusing Holmes of anything which might, conceivably, further distress him. I still considered his recent actions as wonderfully generous and humane. But I knew that Holmes saw then as some kind of failure, and that nothing I could say would alter that. I could only hope that he would find some compensation in a proper recognition of his quite remarkable and revolutionary work upon the potential use of finger prints.

Epilogue

Watson's hope was not fulfilled. Through the assistance of informers, some of the "Dynamiters" were brought to trial, but Holmes' evidence was never used in court. It was considered so revolutionary, that its use might cause the kind of controversy which could cloud the issue. It might lead even to the acquittal of the accused.

In retrospect, that decision cannot be seen as surprising. Holmes' work was years ahead of its time. The use of fingerprints as a part of a system of central criminal records was not adopted by Scotland Yard until 1900. The first recorded case where conviction hung entirely upon the discovery of a bloodstained thumbprint, was in Bengal, in 1898. Methods of making visible, or "developing", invisible prints were still the subject of many forensic papers as late as the 1930s.

Of Sherlock Holmes' reaction to the rejection by both the police and the courts of his own remarkable work, we can guess that it was more than mere disappointment. That it was, in fact, a deep and lasting resentment, would account for one rather curious fact. At no time in Holmes' many future investigations, did he ever seek to use finger print evidence in the solution of a case.

Of Archibold Wilson, we know only this. Watson, in recording *The Adventures of Black Peter*, refers to the eventful year of 1895 and lists among Holmes' successful cases, "his arrest of Wilson, the notorious canary trainer, which removed a plague-spot from the East End of London".